THE BOAT THAT MOOED

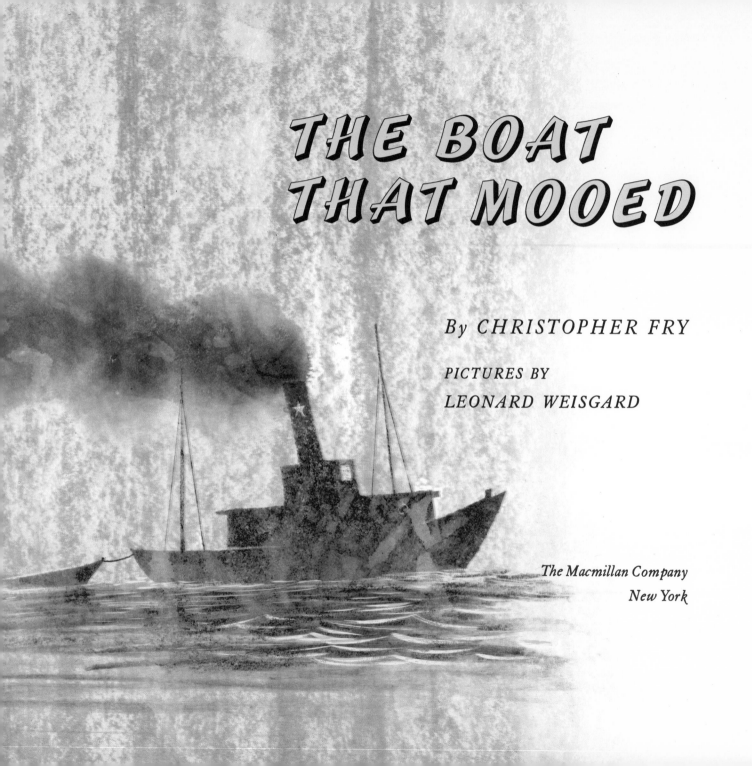

THE BOAT THAT MOOED

By CHRISTOPHER FRY

PICTURES BY
LEONARD WEISGARD

The Macmillan Company
New York

The Macmillan Company, New York.   Collier–Macmillan Canada, Ltd., Toronto, Ontario

Library of Congress catalog card number: 65-15183. Printed in the United States of America

First Printing

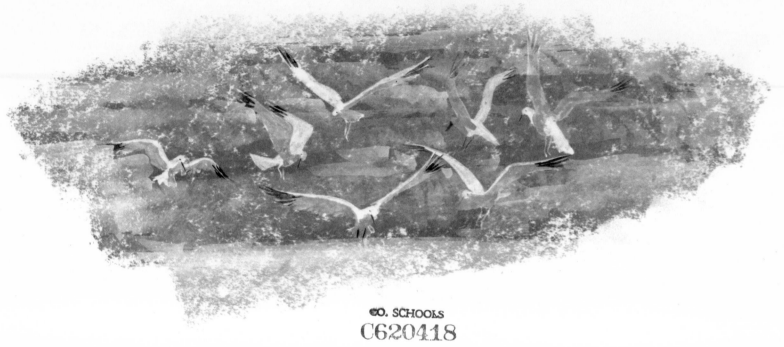

TOM CRUNCH lived on a boat. All around the boat was water. There was water to the right, water to the left, water in front, and water behind. And also water underneath. Up above there was the sky.

Tom Crunch lived with his Uncle Jack, who was fat and sleepy. All day long Uncle Jack sat and fished in the water. Sometimes he was awake, and sometimes he was asleep. It was hard to tell which he was, because he kept his eyes shut all the time, unless he was eating fish. Then he kept his eyes open, because of the bones.

It was a quiet life for Tom on the boat. Uncle Jack did not say much. When he got up he said "Good morning," and when he went to bed he said "Good night."

One day Tom was cleaning a frying pan. He cleaned it so well that he could see his face in it.

"If there had been a cat on the boat," said Tom, "I could have talked to the cat, but let's face it," he said, "there is no cat on the boat. So I suppose," he said, looking at his face in the frying pan, "I suppose I must talk to you."

Then he began to talk to his face in the frying pan.

"I must tell you," he said, "that this is a very dull life. There is nothing to do and nothing to see."

"You can see me," said his face.

"Well, that's not much," said Tom.

"Thank you for being so polite," said his face, sticking out its tongue.

"Don't make faces at *me*, Face," said Tom. And he hung the frying pan on a hook, and went to bed.

Next morning, Tom got up and went to cook his breakfast. He took the frying pan off the hook, and there, in the frying pan, was his face.

"Well," said Tom's face. "Today there really *is* nothing to see."

"What do you mean?" said Tom.

"Go up on deck, and look," said his face.

So Tom went up on deck to look. He looked to the right, and to the left, and in front, and behind, as well as underneath and up above. All he could see was a thick white fog. He could see no sky, and no sun, and hardly any of the boat.

Then Tom called out at the top of his voice, "Uncle Jack! Where are you?"

Nothing happened at first, and then Tom heard his uncle's deep voice calling back.

"Good morning!" said the deep voice.

"Well," thought Tom, "if his voice is there, perhaps *he* is there, too."

So Tom went to find the voice. He went very slowly because the white fog was so thick. It was no good calling out again, because Uncle

Jack had said "Good morning" once, and now he would not say anything else until he said "Good night."

"It might as well be night," thought Tom, "for all I can see." And then he took two more steps, and almost fell over Uncle Jack. What do you think Uncle Jack was doing? He was sitting fishing, in the middle of the thick white fog.

"Uncle Jack," said Tom, "there is nothing to see. There is no water, and no sky, and no sun, and not much boat. It is no good fishing, because there may not be any fish."

But Uncle Jack had said all he had to say, and it was hard to tell if he were awake or asleep.

"I think I had better go and look for everything," said Tom. "I will go and look for the water, and the sky, and the sun, and bring them back here, so that we can have something to look at."

Then Tom went very slowly back along the deck. He knew that the boat had a little boat tied to the end of it. When he got to the end of the big boat he looked for the little boat, but there was only thick white fog.

"I hope you are there, little boat," said Tom, "because I am going to get into you."

So he climbed over the side of the big boat, and let himself down, very slowly. His feet hit something. It was the little boat.

"Oh, hooray!" cried Tom. "So you *are* here, little boat."

Then he untied the rope, and sat down in the little boat. He found the oars to row with, and began rowing away to look for the sky and the sun. He had found the water already. He was rowing on it.

It was funny to row in the middle of a thick white fog. There was no sound at all, except the sound of the oars dipping in the water. And sometimes there was a noise like the mooing of a big cow.

"That must be the noise of another boat. It is telling itself that there is nothing to see," thought Tom.

Tom began to feel very lonely, rowing all alone in a white fog. "I wonder if I shall ever find anything," he said. But he went on rowing, because he wanted so much to find the sky and the sun. All at once he heard an angry squawk close to his ear, and then a white swan came out of the fog.

"Where do you think you're going?" said the swan.

"I am going to look for the sky and the sun," said Tom.

"You might have run me over," said the swan. "Why don't you moo, like any other boat?"

"*Moo!*" said Tom.

Out of the white fog came the noise of another boat, mooing like a cow.

"You see how useful it is to moo," said the swan. "That is how boats talk to each other."

"Please tell me," said Tom. "Where is the sky, and where is the sun?"

"Over there," said the swan, pointing with his neck.

"I don't see anything," said Tom.

"Bad luck," said the swan, and swam away.

Tom felt very lonely again. "I will go and look for the other boat," he thought. "I wonder how far away it is. I will try mooing."

So he dipped the oars into the water, and shouted "Moo!"

"*Moo!*" said the other boat.

"*Moo!*" said Tom.

"*Moo!*" said the other boat.

Tom rowed and mooed, and rowed and mooed, and the other boat mooed back. Each time the other boat mooed, it mooed louder, and louder, and louder, until–

M-O-O-O-O!

It was so loud that Tom nearly fell backwards into the water.

"You don't have to shout," said Tom.

Then Tom saw the other boat. It was right in front of him. He stopped rowing just in time, and called out at the top of his voice: "Don't moo any more! I've found you!"

Then he heard a deep voice singing, and this is what it sang:

> "How many fish
> Are in the sea?
> Some say ten
> And some say three.
> How many are there?
> You tell *me*."

"Hoo-oo-oo!" shouted Tom. "Ho there!"

Then the deep voice began to sing again, and this is what it sang:

"I am the captain of this boat.
   I live upon the water.
   I live with Dan my little dog
   And Ann my little daughter."

"Hoo-oo-oo!" shouted Tom.
Then he heard another voice. It was a little girl's voice.
"Who are you?" said the little girl's voice.

Tom looked up, and he could just see a little girl leaning over the side of the boat, looking down at him in the white fog.

"I am Tom," said Tom.

"I am Ann," said the little girl. "What do you want?"

"I am looking for the sky and the sun," said Tom. "Do you know where they are?"

"I will have to think," said Ann. "Come up on deck while I think. Tie up your boat, and climb up the rope ladder."

So Tom tied up his boat, and climbed up the rope ladder onto the deck. As he climbed up he heard the deep voice singing again, and this is what it sang:

> "Dan my dog says 'Bow-wow-wow.'
> The boat says 'Moo-moo-moo.'
> But in a fog
> What can a dog
> And a little daughter do?"

23

"That is my father singing," said Ann, when Tom stood beside her on the deck. "He is fishing."

"My uncle likes fishing," said Tom. "But he doesn't say much. Does your father say much?"

"He hasn't got much time to say much," said Ann, "because of all the singing. Oh, and this is my dog Dan."

Tom looked down, and there was a white dog.

"Hullo, Dan," said Tom, and Dan licked Tom's face. "I like you very much. But where is the sky and the sun?"

"Wuff! Wuff!" said the dog.

"What does he say?" asked Tom.

"He says we must blow away the fog, and then we shall find the sky and the sun," said Ann.

"It will take a lot of blowing to do that," said Tom.

"Let's try," said Ann. "Ready, steady—blow!"

So they blew very hard all together. They blew and they blew—like this: Phoo-oo-oo! Phoo-oo-oo! Tom blew the white fog. And Ann blew the white fog. And Dan the white dog blew the white fog—like this: Fuff! Fuff! They blew until they had no blow left. Then they sat down on the deck to rest. And all the time Ann's father was singing. "Yo-ho-ho and blow, blow, blow!" he sang. Then they tried again. Phoo-oo-oo! Phoo-oo-oo! Fuff! Fuff!

"It's beginning to go away!" cried Tom. His face was quite red with blowing so hard. "I do believe it's beginning to go away!"

They all blew harder than ever. And Ann's father stopped singing and came to help them. The more they blew, the more the white fog shifted.

First there was a glow, and then there was a gleam, and then the metal on the boat began to shine.

"Hooray!" shouted Tom. "Here is the sun!"

And there it was, the sun itself, looking like a round golden pancake in a dish of steam. And first there was a whiff of blue, and then there was a streak of blue, and then there was a whole patch of blue.

"The sky! The sky!" cried Tom. "It's coming back!"

At that moment the sun sailed into the blue patch and shone so brightly that they all had to shut their eyes. Ann's father began to sing:

"Was there ever a king
With a crown as bright
As the sun in the day
And the moon in the night?"

And they danced around the deck in the sunshine. The sea was dancing too, sparkling, and bobbing, and twisting, and turning, and leaping, and rolling. A fish jumped out of the water, flipped its fins in the sunlight, said, "You can't catch me!" and dived back into the water again. Dan the white dog was so happy that he spun around and around like a top, until he couldn't remember which was his head and which was his tail.

"Enough! Enough!" said Ann's father, when he was tired of dancing.

"Enuff! Enuff!" barked Dan the white dog.

So they all leaned over the side of the boat to look at the dancing sea. They felt as warm as toasted muffins. And the sky was as blue as a blue hyacinth.

28

"Now," said Ann's father to Tom, "where do you live?"

"I live in a boat over there," said Tom. "Just past the big white swan."

"We will go and look for your boat," said Ann's father.

First of all he tied Tom's little boat to the back of the big boat, and then off they went. There was still some white fog in front of them, so Tom and Ann, and Dan the white dog, stood at the front of the boat and blew. And on they went in the sunshine across the water.

"There's the white swan!" said Tom.

The swan looked up, and said, "Oh, so you found the sun all right, then."

"Yes, thank you," said Tom, as they went by.

"And look!" shouted Tom. "There's the boat where I live. And there is Uncle Jack."

And there sure enough was Uncle Jack, sitting fishing. It was hard to tell if he were awake or asleep. By now they had blown all the fog away.

"This is where we will live," said Ann's father. "Right beside your boat."

So the two boats stayed side by side. And one day Tom would go to visit Ann, and the next day Ann would go to visit Tom. And Uncle Jack and Ann's father sat fishing. Uncle Jack said "Good morning" and "Good night," and Ann's father sang. And Dan the white dog ran up and down saying "Wuff! Wuff!"

There was so much to do, and so much to see. Tom and Ann could see the sky, and the sun, and the water, and the boat, and the—well, what else could they see? You tell *me*.